Go Wild!

J. J. Murhall

Illustrated by **Martin Remphry**

a division of Hodder Headline Limited

For Saoirse Ruby, Michael and Alfie
(the angel with the dirtiest face).
De l'audace, encore de l'audace, et toujours de
l'audace. (To dare, still to dare, and ever to dare.)

First published in Great Britain in 2001
by Hodder Children's Books

10 9 8 7 6 5 4 3 2

A Catalogue record for this book is available from the British Library

ISBN 0 340 81728 3

Printed and bound in Great Britain by
The Guernsey Press Ltd, Guernsey, Channel Islands

Hodder Children's Books
A Division of Hodder Headline Limited
338 Euston Road, London NW1 3BH

Department of Unnecessary Buildings

Head Office: Whitehall, London, SW1

Case File No. 502

'Off on your holidays, Mr Rugg?' Oliver Bagshott, Number 5 Condor Gardens' longest-standing tenant, watched as his neighbour from the upstairs flat struggled down the staircase with an extremely bulky holdall.

Two words sprang to mind: distraught and dishevelled. In fact Mr Rugg looked terrible, as if he hadn't slept for a week. His hair was unkempt, his suit was stained and crumpled and his expression was a combination of wild-eyed abandonment and pure rage.

Percival Rugg stared back at him coldly. 'Holidays!' he exclaimed breathlessly. 'I've no time to take a holiday! Don't you realize what they're doing to me?'

Mr Bagshott frowned and pressed himself up against the wall to let Percival Rugg pass. 'Who?' he asked, confused.

'Why, those children, of course,' seethed Percival Rugg. He beckoned for Mr Bagshott to come closer and the friendly neighbour obliged. 'They won't get away with it, though,' he hissed. 'They think they're pulling the wool over my eyes, conning me. But what they don't realize is that I, Percival Rugg, Chief Inspector of the D.U.B. and Best Closer Down of Unnecessary Buildings Regional Gold Medal-winner, 1988, won't be fooled.' He patted the bag protectively. 'In here is everything I need to finally put an end to this little charade.' He unzipped the bag and Mr Bagshott peered tentatively inside. It was full of equipment: camera, binoculars, notebook and pen. There was also a book on bird-watching for beginners, as well as some camouflage gear.

'It looks as if you're off on a field trip,' remarked Mr Bagshott brightly, eager to change the subject. He'd never seen his neighbour look like this before. Come to think of it, he'd never seen anyone look like this before.

'That's exactly what I'm doing,' replied Percival Rugg. 'A trip to the countryside with the enemy. Those little savages can run but they can't hide. Undercover manoeuvres, that's what's needed. A game of cat and mouse with me as the pursuer.' Percival Rugg stared intently at his neighbour. 'I'm going hunting, Mr Bagshott,' he announced coldly. 'Hunting for f-f-fun-loving, rebellious beasts.' Percival Rugg winced and licked his lips. He could barely bring himself to say that word. It left such a bitter taste in his mouth.

'You seem a little tense, Mr Rugg,' the concerned neighbour asked. 'Has someone done something to upset you?'

'Upset! Upset! Of course I'm upset, you fool!' blustered Percival Rugg. 'If I don't get this school closed down soon, my very reputation will be in tatters. My job is already on the line. My superiors want hard evidence that the school isn't being run properly, but I keep on losing my observation notebook and the students' behaviour is so appalling I fear no one will believe me without documentation.'

He grabbed hold of his neighbour's lapel. 'Don't you understand, Bagshott? I could end up like my predecessor, Rodney Archthimble. They said he'd taken early retirement but I know the truth. Archthimble flipped. Lost his marbles. He couldn't take the strain.'

Percival Rugg then gripped both lapels and began to shake Mr Bagshott violently. 'But they won't beat me. Closing down buildings is in my blood. I was born to board up a building! Born to it I say! The only good building in my opinion is one covered in wood and nails with an ACQUIRED FOR DEMOLITION sign stuck outside! I love to board up buildings! Love it, *love it,* LOVE IT, I say!'

Mr Bagshott, however, was unable to respond as he was flung backwards and forwards helplessly like a rag doll. Finally the Chief Inspector calmed down and straightened his tie, before hastily dusting down his neighbour's crumpled jacket.

'Sorry about that, Bagshott,' panted Percival Rugg, running his fingers through his sparse hair, his voice shrill and edgy. 'I'm under a lot of strain at the moment.

Pressures of having such a high-powered job and all that.'

Percival Rugg stared wistfully out of the half-open front door distractedly. Thankful that he was wearing his slippers, Mr Bagshott slowly backed up the corridor, padding soundlessly on the hall carpet towards his flat.

'Today's the day I'll nail them, though,' declared Percival Rugg, stepping forcefully out on to the porch and breathing in the crisp morning air. 'I can feel it in my bones. I just need to keep my cool. Remember that I'm a professional. Trained to work under pressure. Apologies once again for my little outburst, Bagshott. I didn't mean to manhandle you.'

However, his words fell on deaf ears as from behind him there came the sound of a door slamming and a safety chain hurriedly being fastened. The Inspector whirled around. His neighbour was nowhere to be seen.

'Charming,' scoffed Percival Rugg as he headed up the path with his bulky bag. 'Some people can be so rude.' He made a mental note ...

After St. Saviour's assignment seriously consider moving to a more up-market neighbourhood.

From the safety of his locked flat and from behind a pair of net curtains, Mr Bagshott watched as his nutty neighbour scurried up the road looking for all the world like a rat on the edge.

A rat ready to crumble.

A Rugg Rat ready to flip.

St. Saviour's - 7R

REGISTER

2 tsp. Sulphur dipropane.
1 Tbsp. Copper nitrate.
2 Cups. magnesium grape nuts.
1 pinch. Salt.

ASH, Kimberley
BARZOTTI, Daniel
BATHGATE, Hogan
BOW, Crystal
BUTLER, Benjamin
CHENEY, Gemma
CLARK, Tyrone
DEADLY
DREW, Phelim
EARLY, Charles
FISHER, Beasley
HEINZ, Chester
HOPE, Avril
LOVEDAY, Ruby
MONROE, Zoe
NICKS, Stamford
PINKS, Mungo
PRICE, Spencer
RODRIGUEZ, Suzette
STEVENS, Bop
SWELLS, Veronica
TOOMEY, Alfie
TOOMEY, Micky
TOPPER, Lee
WEBB, Marcus
WISE, Scarlett

simmer for 3½ days.

Miss Twine

NOTICE BOARD
Salut! Il fait Très temps.
St. Saviour's school England U.K.
HAS A
Qing Z
NO CRISPS! NO SWEETS
Mr P. RUGG
you lose it
NO SLOUCHING
NO SMILING
NO SINGING
NO SNOGGING!
CLASS 7R
LITTLE TWITTERINGS
FIELD TRIP
WEDNESDAY 9.30.am
Miss Twine
ASTIC
SALE!!
S.O.S.S.S.
FREEDOM MEANS FUN!
F.M.F
PRICES
at Break TIME
SHED
YOUR M8s
L8R!
MATHS -
HISTORY - Mr
ENGLISH - Mr
WOOD WORK - Mr
The Delicate Art of Toa eeding
a talk
Today
A Bore on a Bike
There once was a bore on a bike
Whom certainly nobody liked
NO MAKEUP
NO JEWELLERY
Mr P. RUGG
LAUGHING
NO JOKING
NO F.FUN

Chapter 1
Karaoke Kid

'WOT DO YOU MEAN THE COUNTRYSIDE'S FULL OF KILLER SHEEP?!!' Stamford Nicks was growing more concerned with every mile that was distancing him from the safety of the city.

Beasley helped himself to another sweet from the huge pick 'n' mix bag that his mum had bought him especially for the journey. 'It's true,' he replied adamantly. 'Killer sheep with great big menacing teeth who won't hesitate to attack if you so much as look at them the wrong way.'

Beasley offered his friend the bag but Stamford steadfastly refused. How could he think about eating at a time like this? He'd never been out of the city before in his life. The closest he ever came to a green field was watching football on the telly.

'It's full of birds as big as cats as

well,' continued Beasley, revelling in this far-fetched misinformation. 'There are masses of them. They congregate in trees and are attracted to brightly-coloured, glittery objects.' He looked Stamford sympathetically up and down. His friend was wearing a purple and orange tracksuit that had a mad, multi-coloured pattern spiralling out of control down the arms and legs, plus his entire collection of gold jewellery. 7R's resident bad boy gulped, wishing he'd settled on wearing something a little less eye-catching today instead.

'And you've got to watch out for the cows, too,' Beasley said gravely.

'Why's that?' whimpered Stamford.

''Cause at this time of the year they're changing colour and can be awful grumpy. You'll notice when we get there that they're black and white, sort of patchy looking. Well, normally they're completely black but they're actually in the process of turning white. I'm telling you, Stamford, the countryside's a very dangerous place.' Beasley popped a toffee into his mouth, chewing on it with immense satisfaction. He loved knowing things that Stamford didn't. He also liked winding him up.

'Wot am I going to do, Beas?' implored

Stamford, fiddling nervously with an enormous ingot around his neck. 'My dad has told me I've got to pinch a cow.'

Beasley frowned. 'What does he want you to do that for?' he asked. 'As well as being unpredictable, cows are really expensive to maintain. And besides, you live in a flat. Where you going to keep it? On the balcony? Your mum and dad will have to get rid of all those stolen stereos to make room.'

'It's me mum's birthday next week,' Stamford sighed wearily. 'And as me dad's pinched her nearly everything else, he thought a cow would make a really unusual present. The perfect gift to say "I love yer", he said. My dad always says, "Nicks is our name and nicking is our game." So it don't matter whether it's a cow or a car. If my dad says "Nick it,"' Stamford shrugged, 'I gotta nick it.'

He motioned beneath his seat where there was a length of rope and a packet of porridge oats. 'He's given me a lasso and the porridge is supposed to be the bait.' Stamford shook his head forlornly. 'I wanna go home, Beas. No wonder Deadly didn't want to come. I couldn't get him to leave his dog basket this morning. It was as if he knew I was goin' somewhere really terrible.' The burly boy stared despondently out of the window at the hedges looming over the bus. He felt like he'd landed on another planet where bricks, streetlights and, worst of all, amusement arcades, didn't exist.

Beasley indicated towards the back of the coach where the sound of excited chattering was growing louder. 'Looks like Bop's bought that music machine along again,' he said enthusiastically. 'Fancy joining in? It'll take your mind off things.'

Stamford scowled back at his friend. 'How can I think about havin' a good time when I'm takin' a ride into the unknown,' he snapped sullenly. 'An' besides, I don't want the others thinking I've lost me bottle. I've still got me tough guy image to think about, you know.' He eyed Beasley sternly. 'Say one word about this, Beas, an' I'll feed you to them giant crows and sparrows. Got it?' Stamford leant forward and stared across the aisle at the boy sitting opposite. 'An' that goes for you an' all, Mungo.' Mungo Pinks, however, ignored his friend's threats as he busily scribbled something down. It was a list entitled 'STUFF I REALLY WANT' and he was on item 75 already.

'Oi! Mung-Ears, are you listenin' to me?' shouted Stamford, grabbing a toffee from Beasley's bag and chucking it at him. Beasley looked disgruntled as the toffee bounced off Mungo's head. It was one of his favourites. Below 'Number 75' and the word 'Ferrari' Mungo quickly added 'Number 76 – My own sweet shop.' Then he hastily slipped the paper inside his pocket and grinned across at his friend, his left eye twitching nervously as it always did when he was agitated or about to tell a lie. 'Sorry about that, Stamford. I was just finishing off some homework. What did you say?'

Stamford didn't reply. He wasn't the slightest bit interested in Mungo's excuses. His friend must be losing his lazy touch. Actually *doing* homework was bad enough. But on a school trip? Now that was *really* weird. Stamford thought that perhaps going to the countryside made you do strange things, like turning you into a swot. He shuddered. Perish the thought. It must be all that fresh air.

Stamford stared back out the window and to his horror noticed a flock of birds perched high up in a tree. He trembled again. Even though they were some distance away they looked very, *very* big indeed.

Meanwhile, Mungo Pinks stared silently at the back of Percival Rugg's balding head as the so called *Geography* teacher sat bolt upright, clutching his cumbersome bag. A fortnight ago the phoney tutor had made him an offer he couldn't refuse: anything he wanted. All he had to do was give him vital information about St. Misbehaviour's. Mungo had been mulling it over all weekend and his mind was made up. What harm could it do to accept?

He peered over the top of the seat in front, trying to get a closer look at Percival Rugg's luggage. Perhaps the bag already contained expensive goodies especially for him? Mungo smirked to himself. No one would mock him any more if he rode to school on a better mountain bike than Lee Topper's. That was Number 5 on the list. Or wore the latest trainers, price: £159.99 – Number 9. He could also end up a hero if St. Mis won the School of the Year Award that Mr Rugg had mentioned.

A moment later he and his amazing radar ears were brought straight back down to Earth as the booming voice of Bop Stevens echoed through a microphone and reverberated around the coach. 'Testing. Testing. One. Two. Three.' It was followed by a high-pitched feedback squeal that made Percival Rugg leap up from his seat in alarm.

'What the—!' he spluttered, hardly believing his eyes when he saw that most of 7R had gathered at the rear of the coach where Bop Stevens had set up a mobile karaoke machine on the back seat.

'Fancy doing a turn, Sir?' Bop called out, swinging the microphone around. 'We always like to have a bit of a sing-song when we go on long coach trips.'

Percival Rugg glowered at him, trying to keep his cool. 'Holding a *karaoke* session is hardly the same as having a pleasant, well-organized sing-a-long,' he retorted. 'When I was at school we used to make do with five renditions of "Ten Green Bottles" and then we all had to keep silent with our hands on our heads for the rest of the journey.' The phoney teacher made a mental note ...

Every child wants to be a pop star these days. Ban rock, rap and hippity hop (or whatever the blazes it's called) and make choir practice compulsory.

'When was that song in the charts then?

1957?' asked Lee Topper who was eager to do a turn on the machine. He was brilliant at showing off. 7R laughed as Percival Rugg snorted with disgust and turned his attention towards the Science teacher.

Miss Twine was engrossed in a book entitled *Great Operations of the 21st Century*. Percival Rugg looked in distaste at her travelling companion, Alberta, who was dressed in a bobble hat and gloves. Miss Twine had owned her skeleton 'friend' since medical school and they were inseparable.

'Miss Twine, you must put a stop to this

right now,' snapped Percival Rugg. However, the teacher didn't reply. In fact, Miss Twine seemed oblivious to what was going on around her.

Percival Rugg made a mental note ...

> Science teacher hangs around with a bag of bones. She is definitely gaga. Recommend that she be locked away in the same institution as Rodney Archthimble A.S.A.P.

'MISS TWINE! DID YOU HEAR WHAT I SAID?' bellowed Percival Rugg, clenching his

fists angrily. '7R IS STAGING A POP CONCERT AT THE BACK OF THE BUS! DO SOMETHING!'

He stamped his foot in frustration as Miss Twine dropped her book on the floor before hastily pulling out a pair of earplugs.

'Oh I'm so sorry, Mr Rugg,' she said, sounding flustered. 'I can't hear a thing with these things in. Bop does enjoy bringing his karaoke machine along on trips out. That's why I always wear earplugs. You really should have come prepared, Mr Rugg. You know what boisterous little darlings 7R can be.'

Percival Rugg pulled a disdainful face as she leant around her seat.

'Now, children. Not too loud, please. The inner ear is extremely sensitive to loud noises,' instructed Miss Twine, as Lee started to belt out a rendition of an infamous rapper's latest hit. 'And we don't want to frighten the driver, do we?'

The coach driver rolled his eyes in exasperation as he put his foot down on the accelerator. He'd already had enough shocks for one day – the first being when he'd realized that it was a St. Saviour's school trip that he'd been booked for, and the second being when that skeleton had clattered on board.

*

Twenty minutes later, with Lee Topper still hogging the microphone, the coach careered into the peaceful, picturesque village of Little Twitterings and an old lady, standing quietly outside the post office, couldn't believe her eyes as it passed by. Balloons were flapping out of the windows along with a banner on the back that read 'WARNING! ST. MISBEHAVIOUR'S ON TOUR! PASS WITH CARE!'

Clutching her pension book and looking aghast, she also saw a skeleton in a bobble hat

staring brazenly out of the window at her. And the racket! She'd never heard such a din! It sounded like they were having a party on board.

The lady tutted to herself. What a contrast. Only yesterday another school-hired coach had passed by, heading in the same direction. Those children on board had been extremely well behaved. The woman thought hard for a moment. What had been the name on the front of it? Chaste High? Yes that was it. Nice, neat-looking pupils, all sitting quietly dressed in uniforms with their hair brushed properly. Not like that scruffy lot. She could have sworn they'd been dancing up and down the aisle as well.

'Please, Miss Twine, Crystal Bow's pushed in,' whined Avril Hope as a feisty girl with short bunches, a short skirt and an even shorter fuse elbowed her way determinedly towards the front of the class as 7R congregated in the car park.

Crystal Diamanté Topaz Opal Bow (her parents were millionaire jewellers), 7R's most pampered, privileged pupil, had decided that enough was enough. Somehow she'd ended up next to Chester Heinz when they'd boarded the coach that morning and even though 7R's brainiest kid was OK in small doses, two whole hours of him trying to explain the inner workings of an engine was enough to make a girl do something drastic. The only inner workings Crystal Bow wanted to know about was the mind of Lee Topper and why on earth he didn't fancy her! Which was why she'd trampled all over that whingeing whiner Little Miss Hope*less* just to get to him.

'Looking forward to seeing the countryside?' trilled Crystal to Lee, giving him a fabulous smile. She knew it was a stupid question but hey, she was desperate!

Up ahead Lee Topper scowled and turned up the volume on his portable CD player. Girls were always hassling him. It was an occupational hazard when you were St. Misbehaviour's' most handsome pupil.

'No!' came the short, sharp reply. Lee didn't like the countryside – it mucked up your trainers, it was boring and it smelt funny, too. He glanced irritably at Crystal who was gazing at him like a lovesick monkey and then across at Chester who was now blinking at Crystal through his spectacles like a smitten owl. Lee rolled his eyes. He had no time for such soppy behaviour. Chester loved Crystal. Crystal loved Lee. Lee loved himself. End of story.

Crystal stamped her foot as her dream boy went and plonked himself moodily down on a nearby bench as far away from her as possible. 'Me neither,' she replied with a shrug. Although this wasn't strictly true. She'd actually been looking forward to Miss Twine's field trip all week. She'd had visions of Lee and her sharing a romantic picnic by a babbling brook, or running hand in hand all doe-eyed through a cornfield. Crystal sniffed huffily and checked to see if her nail polish was chipped. Fat chance. 'So far not so good, Crystal baby,' she muttered to herself. Still. She was a girl, so she didn't give up *that* easily. Not ever! No way! No how!

'Children, please,' Miss Twine implored, doing a head count to make sure everyone was present and correct. 'We've come to the countryside for some peace and quiet. To get back to nature.'

Stamford, who'd stubbornly been the last one off the coach, surveyed his surroundings anxiously. He didn't want to get back to nature. He just wanted to get back home.

'I'm *always* at one with nature, man,' Hogan Bathgate, 7R's most environmentally-aware pupil, stepped forward. Dressed in his usual 'saving the world is a dirty business' mucky attire, Hogan put his hands determinedly on his hips. 'It's my job,' he announced earnestly.

Miss Twine nodded in agreement.

‘I know that, Hogan. Which is why I’m putting you in charge of the nature trail today. We need someone who knows his way around the countryside and won’t get lost.’

‘That’s me,’ replied Hogan brightly. ‘The countryside is my second home. I know it like the back of my hand. I can hear the sound of running water a mile away. See grass growing from twenty metres and smell a sheep at fifty paces.’ He stared at his classmates eagerly. ‘We could even camp out here if you like.’ He added proudly, ‘I know how to make a tent out of twigs and cow dung.’

Stamford looked at him suspiciously. ‘Well get sniffin’ then, Bathgate. ’Cause I wanna know if there’s any sheep about,’ he said hesitantly. ‘But I ain’t sleepin’ out here. I’ll get eaten alive.’

‘Don’t tell me you’re a teensy bit scared of the countryside, Stamford?’ asked Bop, trying not to smile.

‘No I ain’t,’ snapped Stamford. ‘I ain’t afraid of nuffink. Wot I mean is I’ll get eaten alive by midges. Those ’orrible insects always bite me. I’ve got delicate skin, see.’ He scratched his nose ring as Bop and the rest of 7R stared at him dubiously.

'Anyway, class,' said Miss Twine. 'I want you to be on your best behaviour whilst visiting Little Twitterings Farm and Nature Reserve today and try not to disturb anyone.'

Percival Rugg scowled to himself. Disturb anyone? These kids disturbed him all the time. They were masters at it.

'I also want you to follow the country code,' continued Miss Twine.

Benjy Butler put up his hand. 'Is that like the highway code? But without the cars?' he asked.

Hogan nodded enthusiastically. 'That's right, man. The country code means not dropping any litter, closing all gates behind you and not worrying the sheep.'

Stamford bit his lip nervously. What on earth was 7R's king of grunge talking about? Worrying sheep? That was the last thing he intended to do. Stamford glanced nervously over his shoulder. He'd run for his life if one of those bleating curly-haired killers even so much as glanced in his direction.

He hurried after Beasley and the rest of the class as they headed off, quickly making their way along a narrow path that led towards the start of the nature trail.

'Slow down, you lot. Wot's the hurry?' complained Stamford, his mammoth jewellery collection clanking like a brass band in the peaceful surroundings.

Bop pointed towards Miss Twine and Percival Rugg as they followed some distance behind. The Science teacher, with Alberta tucked under her arm, was stopping every few metres to inspect the foliage and Percival Rugg kept trying to hurry her along. However, Miss Twine was a thorough scientist and almost every leaf and petal were now coming under her close scrutiny, much to his irritation.

'We need to ditch Miss T and the Rugg Rat for a while,' Bop said determinedly. 'Otherwise, it'll be a riveting afternoon of flower-spotting and examining tree bark. He pointed to sign above his head that read …

**THIS WAY TO VIEW RARE FLORA:
ABARAXNOCIOUS. DO NOT PICK.**

'Not forgetting the Rugg Rat breathing down our necks every five minutes. Did you see the way he's clutching that bag? I'm sure he's up to something.' He stared at his classmates. 'I'm not hanging around to see what it is, though. If he decides to follow us, then I think we should really give him something to write down in his stupid notebook.' Bop grinned. 'I don't know about you lot, but I fancy exploring off the beaten track for a while.'

Everyone agreed, especially Hogan who was beside himself with excitement. He had a surprise up the sleeve of his grubby jumper. 'Well why didn't you say, man? I know a place where we can really have a good time.' He pointed across a field towards the woods.

Lee Topper threw him a distasteful look. 'Listen, Bathgate. You might get your kicks talking to trees, but I don't. I'm not spending an afternoon prancing about in the woods acting like some tree-hugging hippie,' he declared morosely.

Hogan grinned back. 'Don't worry, Lee. Even a city boy like you will enjoy this. Come on.' And he set off determinedly across the field. 7R – with the exception of Stamford, Beasley and Mungo – followed.

'We'll catch you later,' Stamford called after them hesitantly. 'Me, Beasley an' Mungo 'ave got a little business to take care of first.'

Mungo surveyed his friend quizzically. 'What business, Stamford?' asked the oily child, his left eye

twitching tensely. 'Is it something to do with that box of porridge and piece of rope you're holding?'

'Never you mind, Mung-Ears,' snapped Stamford crossly. 'Just follow me and Beasley. I might need to use you as a decoy.'

Mungo looked at him uncertainly. He didn't like the sound of this. Stamford was always using him for things, including target practice. Besides, he had his own business to take care of. He gazed over at Percival Rugg who was glaring in the direction of the absconding class.

'Come back here at once, 7R! You're going the wrong way!' cried the irate Inspector as he watched the wayward pupils race across the field towards the woods. His cries were ignored and he glared down at Miss Twine, who was now on her hands and knees studying a daisy with a magnifying glass. 'Miss Twine, the children have escaped,' he blustered.

'Oh dear, have they?' replied the dissecting-crazy Science teacher, pulling a pair of tweezers and a scalpel from her lab coat top pocket. 'Well never mind, Mr Rugg. I'm sure they'll turn up sooner or later. Besides the fresh air and exercise will do them the world of good.' She plucked a blade of grass and held it up between the tweezers. 'Now this is interesting. Take a look at this, Mr Rugg,' she eagerly remarked.

However, Percival Rugg didn't reply and the meticulous Science teacher looked up to find he was now nowhere to be seen. Miss Twine shrugged, adjusting Alberta's position as she reclined against a tree trunk. 'I don't know what's up with people these days, Alberta. It's rush, rush, rush all the time.' Miss Twine zoomed in on a buttercup with her magnifying glass. 'No one seems to want to stop and smell the flowers any more,' she declared, and with a heavy sigh, plucked up the buttercup and zealously pulled off its petals.

Several minutes later a figure sneaked out from behind a tree further along the path. It was dressed from head to toe in camouflage gear and had a pair of binoculars and a camera slung around its neck.

Tentatively, Percival Rugg looked both ways and seeing that the coast was clear, pulled a mobile phone from the pocket of his flak jacket. Quickly he dialled a familiar number. He hadn't called his secretary at the

Department of Unnecessary Buildings for almost a week now and June tended to worry. After all, this was a woman who fretted even when they ran out of teabags.

Percival Rugg began to trudge across the field as he waited for his secretary to answer. However, there was no reply and the phone clicked on to the answer machine. 'June, where are you?' seethed Percival Rugg resentfully, checking his watch. 'It's 11.45 and twenty-one seconds precisely and you should be working at your desk.'

Percival Rugg gripped his mobile phone furiously. He hated answering machines. You couldn't boss them about.

'Listen June,' he barked into the mouthpiece. 'You're not paid to stand around gossiping all day.' The Inspector narrowed his eyes, his face flushed with anger as he imagined his secretary laughing and joking with his colleagues beside the coffee machine back at the office. 'Listen. When you pick up this message call me straightaway. Otherwise come Monday morning you'll be joining the queue down at the job centre. Goodbye.'

Percival Rugg put his phone back in his top pocket and quickened his pace making a mental note …

Keep an eye on secretary. She may be having too much f-f-fun. Suggest immediate transfer to accounts department down in the basement on my return.

The phoney teacher stomped through the woods muttering crossly to himself. He'd wasted valuable time ringing his absent secretary, because it now appeared that he'd lost those wretched pupils. Percival Rugg stared around in distaste. He wasn't overly fond of the countryside – there weren't any buildings to close, for a start. He made another mental note …

Far too much space in the countryside. Propose intense development in rural areas. High-rise flats. Office blocks. A shopping mall, perhaps? Then close them down and leave them to rot.

Percival Rugg chuckled to himself. 'Build 'em up and board 'em up' – that was going to be his new motto.

The Inspector stopped abruptly as he came to a fork in the path. Uncertain of which branch to follow, he bent down and surveyed the ground, looking for signs of the wayward children.

Suddenly his beady eye homed in on an indentation on the left-hand path. It was a distinctive boot print. He'd recognize it anywhere. That mucky wretch Hogan Bathgate left the same muddy marks all around the school corridors. Percival Rugg chuckled to himself. 'You're a genius, Percy. Trust your old boy scout training not to let you down. Dib. Dib. Dib. Dob. Dob. Dob. Be prepared, Percy my son. Be prepared.' And with that he set off in hot pursuit of his prey.

'Wow! This is well wicked, Hogan!' grinned Benjy Butler, looking around him in amazement.

The rest of the class mumbled in agreement. Hogan had led them on quite a journey through dense head-high bracken (much to Crystal's irritation – it had messed up her hair something rotten). They'd passed along narrow overgrown paths, deep into the very heart of the woods where eventually they'd come across a huge clearing on which an assault course had been built. It was incredible. There was a network of rope ladders leading to an enormous, beautifully-constructed tree house perched high up in a massive oak. A swing bridge was strung across the entire length of the clearing and there was also a pulley with a seat attached, up on a steep bank that led down to a stream.

'This is amazing. A real feat of engineering,' declared Chester, blinking with admiration at his surroundings through his spectacles. 'Who built it?'

'I did,' replied Hogan proudly. 7R stared at him in wonder. 'With the help of my mum and dad and the Save the World Society as well. It's where we spend most weekends, training for the revolution, when we're not out protecting the planet of course.'

'What revolution would that be then?' asked Lee sarcastically. He still hadn't forgiven Hogan for scaring him on the 'Live Like a Roman' trip the other week. 'The revolt against revolting kids who don't ever wash?' he sneered.

Hogan ignored his fellow pupil's remarks. 'Come the revolution,' he announced, climbing up on to the bank to make one of his famous speeches, 'and all animals and trees will breathe a sigh of relief again. Being a vegetarian will be made compulsory and trees will grow freely without fear of being chopped down.' Hogan stared dreamily across the clearing, tears welling up in his eyes. He was passionate about saving the planet.

Lee rolled his eyes in exasperation as he went off to explore. He could never give up eating burgers, and trees in his opinion were just overgrown bushes that blocked out the light.

The rest of 7R dispersed, all eager to test out this remarkable construction, with the exception of Bop. He had an uneasy feeling. Having a good time at St. Mis was becoming more and more difficult. Back at school Percival Rugg was always sneaking up behind them or scribbling stuff discreetly into his new notebook. There was now a price to pay for having fun and Bop knew instinctively that the Rugg Rat wouldn't be far behind them.

He looked around at his classmates, whooping with delight as they careered down

the pulley landing on top of each other in the stream. Others were swinging like chimps across the clearing, whilst some had laid out their packed lunches and were relaxing in the autumn sunshine.

The S.O.S.S.S. (Save Our School from Spoilsports) members had recently come up with a school motto and emblem which was very apt for St. Misbehaviour's. It was a picture of a toad (their Head Teacher's favourite animal) jauntily wearing a party hat on his head. Below him were the initials F.M.F. and above his head were the words 'FREEDOM MEANS FUN'. They'd shown it to M*sss* Bicep-Tricep and she'd thought it looked splendid, deciding that the emblem would now be used on everything connected with the school, including football kits and headed notepaper.

Bop smiled to himself. FREEDOM MEANS FUN. 7R were certainly living up to their new school motto this afternoon and he'd decided that nothing and no one was going to stop them.

He called Benjy over and the small boy hurried towards his friend, grinning breathlessly. 'You've got to have a go, Bop. That pulley thing is wicked. It's the fastest ride I've ever been on.'

Bop put an arm around his shoulders. 'Sorry to stop you, Benj. But we need to call an urgent meeting. I've got a feeling that the Rugg

Rat's sniffing around. We need a plan. Something that will stop him in his tracks once and for all. Go and get Chester for me first. I need his advice.'

Benjy nodded. 'OK. Have you got any ideas, Bop?'

Bop Stevens grinned back at his friend. 'It'll take a bit of work and Chester's brain power, but I think we can stop that phoney freak once and for all.'

Benjy grinned back at his friend. He knew Bop wouldn't let them down. He was, after all, the Mastermind of Ideas.

Chapter 3

Lock Up Your Cows

'Run faster, Beasley! Faster!' Stamford stood in the middle of the field, glaring as his chunky friend – clutching a box and swinging a lasso – chased after a cow. Round and round in circles they went, with Beasley leaving a trail of porridge oats in his wake as he tried to coax the creature – to no avail.

'It's no good, Stamford,' he panted. 'I can't catch it. I think your tracksuit might be scaring it.'

Stamford scowled at him and then down at his lurid outfit. 'Well, try harder,' he snapped. 'I told you, my dad's gonna kill me if I don't bring one home.'

Beasley stopped to catch his breath. 'Can't we get your mum something else instead? How about a nice bunch of flowers?' he said brightly. 'Or maybe *you* could have a go.' He held out the length of rope and the crumpled box.

Stamford shoved his hands in his tracksuit pockets protectively. 'No way!' he replied. 'I ain't gettin' anywhere near one of them 'orrible things. You said they was unpredictable an' now I see wot you mean.' He glared back across the field. 'Where's Mungo got to, anyway? We should make him 'ave a go. He said he was going back to the coach for his anorak but he's been gone ages. I reckon he's done a runner. Trust him to run a mile at the first sign of danger.' He looked apprehensively back at the cow, which was now contentedly munching on some grass.

Suddenly, Stamford perked up and put a finger to his lips. 'OK, Beas. I've had an idea,' he whispered. 'We'll change tactics. Ditch the porridge 'cause I don't think cows eat breakfast cereal. Wot you gotta do is sneak up behind it and grab its tail. Then you can throw the rope over its 'ead and bingo! We've got ourselves a big furry birthday present wot moos!'

Beasley looked at him dubiously. Since when had Stamford Nicks, city boy and countryside despiser, become such an expert on cattle rustling? 'OK. I'll give it a go,' he conceded. It was no use backing down where Stamford was concerned. He'd never let you off the hook. Mungo had had the right idea by doing a disappearing act for a while. Beasley pulled his hat flaps down determinedly and then began to tiptoe across the field.

'Atta boy, Beas!' hissed Stamford following slowly behind. 'Easy does it.'

Beasley approached the cow tentatively, then ever so slowly, he stretched out a hand and grabbed hold of its tail. The cow looked up from its lunch nonchalantly, glanced at Beasley and then immediately bolted.

'Hold on, Beas! Don't let go!' hollered Stamford as Beasley Fisher, cattle thief and now part-time cowboy, began to run, clutching the tail with both hands, like a rodeo star.

'I can't hold on much longer!' cried Beasley as the cow began to trot faster, heading towards an open gate.

'Lasso it!' shouted Stamford, chasing after him.

Beasley let go of the tail with one hand and began to swing the rope around his head with the other, before throwing it in the direction of the cow's head. He missed. The cow trotted faster, through the gate and into the next field, before Beasley finally let go. He hadn't run so fast since their History teacher, Mr Bateau, had chased him and the rest of 7R around the playground in a rage a few weeks ago.

Stamford ran up behind him. 'You almost 'ad it! Wot did you let go for?' he complained breathlessly.

Beasley scowled from beneath the brim of his hat. 'You try holding on to the back end of a two-ton runaway cow!' he replied sullenly. 'I ain't Superman, you know.'

Stamford didn't reply. He was now staring across the field fearfully, his face ashen.

Beasley frowned. 'What's up, Stamford? You've gone all pale.'

Stamford gulped and pointed a shaky finger across the field. 'K-k-killer sh-sh-sheep! O-o-over th-th-there,' he stammered.

Beasley followed his friend's gaze. It was true. The whole area was dotted with fluffy, off-white, four-legged creatures, hundreds of them – and they were all staring straight at Stamford Nicks.

A meeting of the S.O.S.S.S. society had been called by Bop in the tree house. Everyone had come along. (Crystal thought that being stuck half-way up a tree with Lee Topper would be great, a bit like a Tarzan film, where she could play the part of his glamorous girlfriend, Jane.)

Everyone agreed that they were heartily sick of Percival Rugg and his interfering ways.

'I hate the way he picks on us,' moaned Kimberly Ash.

'All the time,' added her best friend, Suzette Rodriguez.

'For the slightest, teeniest little thing,' concluded Kimberly.

The students of 7R mumbled in agreement.

'He's spoiling our lessons as well,' grumbled Hogan. 'You know that tree sculpture I'm making in Art? My "Homage to the Mighty

Oak" made out of recycled stuff?'

Everyone nodded. How could they miss it? You could hardly get through the classroom door it was so big now, and it also reached the ceiling.

'Well, the Rugg Rat says it's not art, it's rubbish. He's told me to dismantle it and chuck it out before the next lesson.' Hogan sighed. 'I've been building that since the beginning of term. It's one of my greatest creations, apart from this place, of course,' he added, looking around the tree house with pride. 'He reckons I should be sketching bowls of fruit or trying my hand at some lino-cutting. But that's so *boring*.'

'Yeah. Just like him,' replied Benjy morosely. Everyone nodded again, and began to vent their complaints about Percival Rugg and his meddling ways – from his insistence that the graffiti wall be painted over, to not allowing music to be played in the common rooms at break times. His lists of rules, pinned up all over the school, were becoming endless. No crisps, no sweets, no chewing gum, no mobiles, no chatting in the corridors, no football in the playground, no trainers, no drinks machines, no slouching, no singing, no smiling, no snogging (I should be so lucky, Crystal Bow had thought when she'd read *that* one), no after-school clubs (except chess), no make-up, no jewellery ('Dream on,' Stamford had laughed), no trendy bags, no trendy anything, no laughing, no joking, NO F-F-F-FUN! On and on the rules went in an endless round of nagging.

Not that anyone took a bit of notice of the phoney Geography teacher, but it was certainly becoming harder to get away with things. One slip and there Percival Rugg would be, spying like a secret agent and scribbling frantically into his latest notebook.

Even M*sss* Bicep-Tricep, St. Misbehaviour's' normally unfazed Head Teacher, was growing a little concerned. 'He's proving a tough nut to crack,' she'd declared at an after-school emergency meeting held last week. 'Our dearly departed Rodney Archthimble had already left with his tail between his legs by now. You need to work harder, children. Have *more* fun. Be louder. Be cheekier. Really get on his nerves. Then perhaps Mr Slugg will get the message and slither off back to that dreadful place from whence he came.'

'What M*sss* B said was right,' declared, Bop, who was seated alongside Chester and Benjy at the head of an oblong table, made out of tree bark. 'We've got to wind the Rugg Rat up even more. So while you lot were out there having fun, Chester and I have been thinking and we've come up with a plan.' Bop pointed at some sheets of notepaper spread out over the table. 'One that will hopefully make the Rugg Rat see sense and give up.'

The class eagerly gathered round, straining to get a look at the drawings. Chester had drawn sketches of the assault course, indicating key points dotted around the area showing lengths of rope. There was also a picture of a bucket hanging above a matchstick figure with a moustache and glasses.

Lee pointed towards it. 'I can see that's the Rugg Rat. But what's this?' he asked. 'It looks like some kind of a trap.'

'Ooh! Let's have a look,' said Crystal, once again shoving Avril Hope out of the way. She liked the sound of being trapped somewhere with Lee. He wouldn't be able to keep running away from her then.

'It's my *rat* trap, actually,' Chester replied proudly, glancing over his shoulder to see if Crystal was impressed. 'I've based it on a board game I used to have when I was a little kid. You had to build a construction out of various pieces in order to ultimately catch a plastic mouse. I can't remember what it was called, but it was fun at the time. Only my dad said it wasn't very educational and he confiscated it,' he added dejectedly.

Bop patted him sympathetically on the back. He'd been to Chester's house. It resembled a musty old museum crammed full of encyclopaedias and chemistry sets, but not much else.

'Well never mind, Ches,' he said brightly. ''Cause now you've got a chance to make a life-sized one.' He rubbed his hands together.

'Right, gang. Let's get to work. I want you all to gather outside where we'll show you what's to be done. It'll take a bit of effort and we need to work fast but it'll definitely be worth it. Make as much noise as you can 'cause we need the Rugg Rat to know exactly where we are. If we can pull this off, old Percy pain in the neck will get such a shock he'll leg it back to the D.U.B. faster than you can say our new school motto. Which is?' Bop cupped his hands to his ears and grinned.

'FREEDOM MEANS FUN!' came the resounding reply, and everyone laughed as they prepared to set about building a rat trap for the world's biggest rat.

Chapter 5

Highly Strung

'Stupid, stupid children,' Percival Rugg muttered smugly to himself. 'No wonder I can track you lot down with all the noise you're making. You'd never make it as undercover professionals like me with all that racket.'

As he fought his way through the dense undergrowth towards the source of the sound, he made a mental note …

> Suggest introduction of 'Quiet Time' where all children must not speak for at least a week. Failure to comply will result in immediate imprisonment.

Percival Rugg let out a woeful moan as he remembered his own internment – arrested on that dreadful toga trip and thrown unceremoniously into a police cell. He grunted and narrowed his eyes resentfully. If he had his way he'd capture these particular kids and then throw away the key for ever. He listened carefully. The whoops and cries were definitely coming from a northerly direction, deep in the heart of the woods. 'Keep on laughing, 7R,' he sniggered. *'Whilst you still can.'*

The meddling Inspector quickened his pace, clutching his camera protectively. 'You should have thought about photographic evidence at the start of this assignment, Percy. After all, the camera never lies.' He chuckled as he imagined his colleagues' astonished faces back at the D.U.B. when various incriminating snapshots of 7R up to no good landed on their desks first thing on Monday morning.

Suddenly however, Percival Rugg stopped in his tracks. He was confused. A moment ago he'd been following the distinctive sounds of children's laughter but now it was deathly quiet. The Inspector frowned, parted some ferns between his fingers, and peered through them, his long prying nose twitching in anticipation.

In the distance he could see a large clearing with what appeared to be some sort of adventure playground and assault course built on it. 'Hmm. The perfect location for a bunch of kids with mischief on their minds,' he muttered gleefully. The only trouble was the place seemed to be deserted. He zoomed his binoculars upwards and also saw a stunning tree house, and frowned.

He began to edge his way slowly towards the clearing. The only sounds he could hear now were his own shallow breath and the occasional crack of a twig beneath his feet. Even the birds seemed to have stopped singing. Percival Rugg stepped into the clearing and looked around. Although it was deserted he had the strangest feeling – the feeling he'd had that Sunday when he'd first visited the wretched school – that he was being watched.

Then the Inspector noticed an object lying in the middle of what appeared to be a circle of rope and he hurried over to it. Curiously, he picked up the distinctive, shabby jumper that he was sure belonged to that eco-worrier kid, Hogan Bathgate. Tucked in the sleeve was a crumpled piece of paper that also looked familiar. Percival Rugg snatched it out and frowned. It was the same type of paper that he always used in his notebooks. Carefully he unfolded it and spread it out between his fingers. His eyes widened in amazement as he realized that although the ink had run, he was actually staring at his own neat handwriting, and reading his own contemptuous words on the piece of paper that he'd so stupidly misplaced all those weeks ago: 'Sunday, 12 November 11.08 am. First impressions of earmarked *doomed* location.' He flipped it over where written on the back in childish felt-tip scrawl it simply said: 'WHERE'S QING ZANG?'

Percival Rugg grimaced, staring around at his deserted surroundings. This had obviously been planted here for him to find. He screwed it up angrily. He'd been rumbled. In fact, these kids had probably known all along that he wasn't a *real* Geography teacher. He began to shake indignantly. 'You despicable little monsters,' he seethed. 'Show yourselves this instant.'

However, there was complete silence. High up in the trees, behind the surrounding bushes and hidden in the tree house, 7R silently watched their enemy, waiting eagerly for Bop's signal.

Bop Stevens, his face now smeared with war paint from Crystal Bow's make-up bag, peered carefully over the tree house window ledge. Beside him was his second-in-command and best buddy, Sergeant Benjy Butler. Field Marshall Chester Heinz and Captain Hogan Bathgate were crouched in anticipation on the other side whilst some other recruits from 7R's 644 Squadron on Operation Catch-a-Rat were huddled behind him.

'What's he doing?' whispered Hogan excitedly. He'd dreamt of this day, when he'd be able to ambush an enemy. Now, how radical was that? The Save the World Society would be so proud of him when they found out that he'd spared the world from a spoilsport.

'We just need him to take one more little step forward,' hissed Bop. 'And then he'll be in the exact spot for Operation Sludge Bucket.'

The others tried not to laugh as Bop picked up a small stone that was lying on the wooden floor beside him and chucked it out of the window.

Percival Rugg frowned as the stone bounced off a nearby tree trunk. 'Who's there? Show yourselves,' he demanded, taking a single step forward.

Then Bop gave a burst of four short shrill whistles and from high up in the

tree opposite where the pulley was attached, a large wooden bucket swung leisurely backwards and forwards. Lee began to pull on one end of the rope and it began to slide silently towards an unsuspecting Percival Rugg. Then Lee tugged again on the rope and the bucket stopped abruptly, directly above Percival Rugg's head.

The Inspector, sensing something, stared slowly up in disbelief. 'What the—?' he said in

surprise as the bucket tilted and then gradually tipped up, its contents oozing out and over his astonished face. It was one of Hogan's rural recipes. A mixture of mud and cow dung. Percival Rugg spluttered and wiped the muck from his face. 'How *dare* you!' he seethed, his mouth full of manure. At which point Lee let the bucket go and it landed on his head. Percival Rugg tried to pull it off as he swayed from side to side, the gungy mixture stuck fast.

'Quick, Chester,' urged Bop. 'Proceed with Operation Catch-a-Rat. Now!'

Chester rubbed his hands together and pushed his glasses up his nose in concentration as he prepared for the most delicate part of the operation. 'Easy does it,' he said, carefully pulling on the circle of rope that surrounded Percival Rugg's feet. Then he yanked on it sharply and the rope tightened around the Inspector's skinny ankles. Quickly, the other children also grabbed the end of the rope and pulled hard.

In an instant, the phoney teacher was whisked off his feet and hoisted up into the air. The bucket fell off with a squelching sound as Percival Rugg dangled upside down. 'Right, that's it!' he bellowed, his face a mask of drying cow dung. 'Get me down this instant!'

The children began to emerge from their various hiding places and gather around him.

'Oh Mr Rugg. What a mess,' said Crystal Bow sweetly. She turned her head at an angle to get a better look at the phoney teacher's flustered face. 'Still. I'm sure the others busybodies back at the D.U.B. will understand when you go back to your *real* job smelling like a farmyard.'

'Don't mess with St. Misbehaviour's, Mr Rugg,' Bop declared. 'It can lead to trouble.'

'You won't get away with this, you know,' seethed Percival Rugg, struggling furiously against his bindings.

'But it looks like we already have, Mr Rugg,' said Crystal with a slight shrug. She pushed him lightly and the phoney teacher swung backwards and forwards like a pendulum. The class began to wander away.

'Where are you going?' demanded Percival Rugg. 'You can't leave me suspended like this!'

'Oh yes we can,' said Bop as he headed off into the woods. 'At least for a while anyway.' He turned and grinned at the Inspector. 'Don't you realize, Mr Rugg? We can do anything! We're St. Misbehaviour's!'

Hogan jumped up on to the bank. 'Power to the pupils!' he yelled at the top of his voice. His words echoed around the woods and then fell deathly silent. The children waited for a moment in the stillness. It was as if the very trees themselves were listening to him.

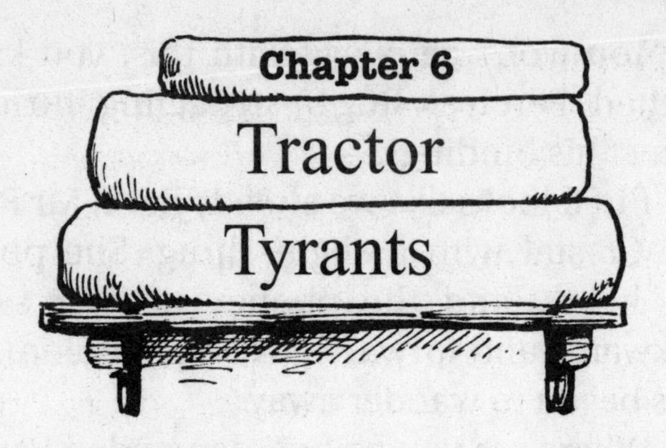

'But I thought you said you could drive!' wailed Beasley Fisher, covering his face with one hand and clinging on to his friend for dear life with the other, as Stamford Nicks crashed the tractor through his fourth hedge of the afternoon and chugged across yet another muddy field.

'Stop panicking will yer! I can!' Stamford hollered over his shoulder as he wrestled with the wheel. 'I told yer. Drivin's easy! All you gotta do is watch the road!' He put his foot down on the accelerator as they drove over a particularly large bump. 'The only trouble is there ain't no roads to follow out here!' He pointed across the field where a dirt track and a signpost could be seen up ahead. At the end of it, in the distance, was an imposing-looking farmhouse. 'That's why I'm heading over there. Once I get on a proper surface I'll be able to steer straight,' he shouted.

Beasley peeped out from between his fingers as Stamford veered off towards it. What on earth had he got himself into? First cattle rustling and now a spot of T.D.T.A. (otherwise known as Taking and Driving a Tractor Away). And all because Stamford had panicked, thinking he was about to be chased by a flock of sweet harmless sheep. Beasley shut his eyes as they bounced across the open field. He'd decided that if he came through this little escapade unscathed he'd find himself a more sensible friend to hang around with. One who wasn't a criminal or quite so stupid would do for a start.

'Uh oh. Hold on tight, Beas!' cried Stamford apprehensively. 'There's another gang of them dangerous woolly jumpers lying in wait up ahead. I'm going to have to put me foot down and drive straight through 'em.'

Beasley clung on desperately as Stamford, hunched over the wheel, headed towards them determinedly, making the peacefully-grazing sheep scatter in all directions.

'Woo! Woo! Woo! Wicked!' exclaimed Stamford, bouncing excitedly up and down on his seat and clicking his fingers delightedly in the air. 'See the way they legged it, Beas? Those furry-faced cowards! They ain't so tuff now Stamford's in the driving seat! Do you know wot? I'm starting to enjoy the countryside.' He grinned. ''Ave you noticed the way there's no one around to tell you off for breakin' the law? I might even move here. I bet there's loads of stuff to nick apart from cows, if you look hard enough.'

Beasley implored, 'But don't you think we ought to stop now?' as Stamford drove the tractor over a cattle grid and through a gate that lead to the farm. 'This tractor probably belongs to the owner of this place and the farmer won't be to happy when he finds out we've stolen it.'

'I think we might be a little too late for that, Beas. Take a look behind you. It's not sheep wot's after us. It's some red-faced geezer with a great big fork!'

Beasley glanced over his shoulder, where an extremely irate man was now chasing after them. He was obviously a farmer because he was wearing wellingtons and was brandishing a rather lethal-looking pitchfork. 'You'd better stop, Stamford. He looks ever so cross,' insisted Beasley

with trepidation. Stamford shook his head and put his foot down on the accelerator instead. 'No way! I'm not hanging around for some loony farmer to catch me,' he yelled above the noise of the engine. 'Who knows wot sort of punishment they hand out for messin' about in the country? Tractor nickin' is probably a really serious offence in these parts. We could end up doing a ten-year stretch or even life with nothing to look forward to except muckspreading or feeding chickens every day.'

However, before Beasley could reply, an almighty shout echoed through the air, making a flock of birds take flight. Stamford looked skyward uneasily in case they were also heading his way and then anxiously behind him.

The farmer shook his fist and then shook his pitchfork wildly in the air again.

'Oh no. That giant fork looks well sharp!' wailed Stamford. 'You're right, Beas. The countryside is a very dangerous place. I've changed me mind. I wanna go back to the city where a kid can be safe!'

Beasley rolled his eyes in desperation as the farmer shouted at the top of his voice and waved his fist once again. 'He's *warning* us to stop,' he cried, holding on to his hat as it nearly blew off.

'All right, all, right, I'm turnin' myself in. I don't want a pitchfork in me pants,' said Stamford, putting both hands in the air.

Beasley breathed a sigh of relief, before realizing to his horror that Stamford wasn't actually holding on to the steering wheel any more. 'Look out!' he cried as the tractor trundled out of control into the courtyard of the farm, straight through a washing line of clothes and out the other side.

'Help! Wot's happenin'? The countryside's well weird. It's gone dark all of sudden!' cried Stamford, waving his arms wildly around in the air.

'That's because you've got a cardigan stuck to your face!' Beasley shouted, pulling the offending article off just before the tractor careered into a duck pond.

When the two boys emerged a few minutes later, dripping wet, they came face to face with the grim-faced farmer. Stamford gave him a feeble smile and handed him the sodden cardigan. 'Sorry about the mess, mate,' he grinned sheepishly.

'Mess! It's more than a mess!' roared the farmer, still brandishing his pitchfork menacingly. 'You've ruined my tractor, not to mention my washing! Everyone knows that farmers have a hard life as it is. But let me tell you, it's even harder when your washing-machine breaks down at five in the morning! I had to wash this lot by hand, just before I did the milking!' He pointed at his tractor. 'That vehicle's got dodgy brakes and shouldn't be driven by amateurs, especially children! Didn't you hear me calling you to stop?'

Beasley looked ashamed as Stamford shrugged. 'Yeah, but we was in danger. You won't believe the day I've had. Killer sheep after me, runaway cows, birds as big as cats.' Stamford shrugged and shook his head in admiration. 'It takes a lotta bottle to live in the countryside, Mister. I reckon you must be braver than the bravest person I know.'

The farmer eyed him up and down, although he was beginning to warm to the boy. He'd never been called 'brave' before. Hard-working and resilient, yes. But courageous, never. 'And who's that then – your father I suppose?' he replied crossly.

'No way!' said Stamford, sounding amazed. 'I'm talking about me mum. She ain't afraid of nothin'. You could put her in the countryside and every creature would run a mile when they saw her, including you,' declared Stamford proudly, full of admiration for his mum.

Beasley nodded in agreement as he thought about Mrs Nicks stalking the mean streets of the city, scaring the pants off everyone she ever met. Big bad Mrs Nicks! She was indeed a fearsome, formidable lady.

Hidden behind a hedge, his anorak securely fastened right up to his chin, Mungo Pinks watched silently as his fellow pupils headed off noisily through the woods. When the coast was clear, he gingerly stepped out into the clearing and then hurried towards the dangling Geography teacher who eyed him angrily.

'You, boy! Get me down this instant!' demanded Percival Rugg, wriggling in frustration.

Mungo stepped closer and stared up at him. 'I've brought my list,' he announced eagerly, pulling it from his anorak pocket.

'List? What list?' snapped Percival Rugg. He gazed at Mungo's sheet of paper warily. He'd had quite enough of notes and their contents for one day.

'My list of stuff that you're going to

give me in exchange for information about St. Mis, of course,' replied Mungo huffily. Surely Mr Rugg couldn't have forgotten? Mungo had thought of little else for weeks. His left eye began to twitch enthusiastically. 'I've got loads to tell you. For the right price though,' he added shrewdly.

A bitter smile flickered across the phoney teacher's face as he realized that this stupid boy could quite possibly be his last hope of success. Even though he felt as if his head was about to explode, Percival Rugg knew he needed to keep his cool, to get this little twit on his side. 'Ah yes, the list,' he remarked brightly. 'Well, if you just get me down first, Mungo, then perhaps we can talk business.'

'What? The business of how much *stuff* you're going to give me?' replied Mungo, sticking his chin out brazenly. The slimy boy trusted no one, especially not Percival Rugg. No wonder his classmates had gone to so much trouble to string this so-called Geography teacher up. Mungo thought that Lee Topper's bucket trick had been really hilarious.

Percival Rugg nodded vigorously as he swung perilously about. 'Yes, that's right. Now just get me down, quickly now, Mungo.'

Mungo nodded and then hurried off, following the length of rope as it led to the base of the oak tree, up the trunk and into the tree house. 'Won't be long,' he shouted as he climbed the ladder and stepped into the house.

Percival Rugg muttered incoherently to himself. It was just his luck to have the world's dimmest child working for him.

Inside the house Mungo surveyed his surroundings, very impressed. Perhaps he could have a tree house like this one in his own back garden? Now, that would be really great. He hastily pulled out his sheet of paper and added it to the long list before untying the rope.

Down below Percival Rugg slumped to the ground as the rope slackened. He quickly untied his ankles and leapt up. He had no time to lose before dopey boy returned with the incriminating information. He'd decided that he still needed photographic evidence and the Inspector began to snap away with his camera. The rope, the bucket, the crumpled note. He even took a snapshot of his own muddy face.

'OK. What do you want to know?' said Mungo, strolling over to him. 'Only I can't be too long 'cause Stamford and Beasley will wonder where I've got to,' he added hastily.

Percival Rugg put the camera behind his back and smiled insincerely at the boy. 'As I told you on the swimming trip the other week, if St. Saviour's is going to have the remotest chance of winning this award then I need facts for my nomination,' he said slyly. He smirked to himself. The only facts that this kid could give him about such a despicable place just *had* to be negative ones.

Mungo took a deep breath as he prepared to divulge what he'd found out. 'OK. Here goes. Facts about St. Mis in exchange for item Number 1 on my list – a jumbo jet,' announced Mungo.

Percival Rugg stared back in amazement as Mungo held up a finger. 'First: it was founded in 1959 by M*sss* Bicep-Tricep, although the building itself dates back to 1907, the toilets possibly even earlier. Second fact: St. Saviour's is the world's first school where teachers are employed on personality rather than qualifications.'

Mungo took another deep breath and concentrated hard. He'd been memorizing these facts all over the weekend from the glossy prospectus that he'd obtained from M*sss* Bicep-Tricep's office. It was the most homework that he'd ever done. 'Fact number 3: Even though our exam results are amongst the poorest in the country, more of our pupils have gone on to make their fortunes in the field of arts than any other school, ever. These include a Booker Prize-winning bus conductor, as well as six bestselling novelists; four Hollywood film stars; three artists exhibiting at the Museum of Modern Art in New York, the Guggenheim and the Tate Gallery in London; eight dancers currently starring in West End musicals and a boy band that have had four consecutive number one hits, both here and in America. They've also won two Brit awards and a Grammy at the tender age of seventeen. Shall I go on?' Mungo stared at Percival Rugg quizzically.

The Inspector nodded, his head swimming

as Mungo's voice droned on.

'Fact number 4. This is for item 2 on my list – my own penthouse. Even though the school has gone through various disasters over the years including fires, floods, an unexploded World War Two bomb found in the basement and an attempt by the D.U.B. to close it down—' he eyed Percival Rugg suspiciously and the phoney teacher guiltily lowered his eyes, 'St. Saviour's continues to thrive under the guidance of its ever popular Head Teacher, M*sss* Cynthia Bicep-Tricep O.B.E., C.B.E. and B.T.E.'

Percival Rugg put up his hand. 'Hold on a minute. What does B.T.E. stand for?' he frowned.

'Best teacher ever!' smiled Mungo. 'We made that one up. Now for item 3 – a shopping spree to the value of £3,000.'

Mungo took another deep breath as he prepared to tell the Inspector about all the other investigations and lawsuits that the school had somehow managed to escape.

'Hold it! Hold it!' interrupted Percival Rugg. 'Don't you have any facts about St. Saviour's that are more, how shall I put it,' the Inspector gritted his teeth, '*more damning*? I need some information about what the pupils get up to after school. Vandalism, perhaps? Being cheeky to their elders? I'll certainly make it worth your while,' he added enticingly.

'Oh, you mean like when Stamford goes and visits the old people's home in the city centre?' smiled Mungo knowingly.

Percival Rugg squealed with delight and nodded enthusiastically. 'Yes, that's right,' he gasped, his eyes glinting with anticipation. 'And what does he get up to there? Terrorizing the old folks and robbing them of their belongings, I assume?' he added, almost beside himself with excitement. This was just the sort of evidence that he needed. A young thug on the loose in a retirement home.

Mungo frowned at Percival Rugg who was starting to quiver with expectation. 'No way,' replied Mungo. 'Why would he want to do that? He takes Deadly along to cheer them up. They really like Stamford, but they *love* that dog.'

Percival Rugg clenched his fists as he thought of that slobbering mutt who'd brazenly eaten his mobile phone and precious notebook. The dreadful beast!

'Stamford's got a lot respect for old people,' Mungo continued. 'Both his grandparents are currently doing time in prison. And he's really proud of them. They're the country's oldest inmates!' Mungo shook his head adamantly. 'No, Mr Rugg. Stamford would never break into an old person's house.'

Percival Rugg reached for his notebook and pen. 'Ah! But you're saying that Stamford Nicks is *sometimes* a common or garden burglar?' he quipped with his pen poised ready for an exclusive scoop.

Mungo gulped and thought about what Stamford would do to him if he grassed him up. 'He used to be,' he added hurriedly. 'But he's given all that sort of stuff up now. He's decided to turn over a new leaf and become a good kid. In fact, he's even thinking about joining the after-school chess club,' remarked Mungo. His left eye twitched vigorously. 'Anyway. Talking of stuff, Mr Rugg,' he said, eager to change the subject, 'what about mine? I've given you some background info about St. Mis, and now I want my rewards.'

Percival Rugg stared back at him calculatingly. 'You've given me ordinary facts that I could have gleaned from a book or by reading the local paper,' he scoffed. 'They're hardly the secrets of the century.' Percival Rugg surveyed the boy coldly as an important question popped into his mind. One that had been puzzling him since he'd first arrived at the school. 'However, I will give you something if you answer me *one* question.' He leant closer and Mungo stepped back a little. 'I want to know the whereabouts of a certain place. A place called Qing Zang. Does it exist, child? Or is it just another one of Year 7's fanciful lies intended to wind me up?'

Mungo stepped further back, shaking his head fearfully from behind the collar of his anorak. 'Ask me anything except that,' he gasped. 'Anyone who divulges the answer to *that* question will be expelled instantly from the school.' Mungo looked around him uneasily. 'You see, before a pupil can be admitted to St. Mis they have to find out where Qing Zang is. It's a test that M*sss* Bicep sets for all prospective pupils,' he said gravely.

'Ah! So it *is* a real place, then?' said Percival Rugg excitedly. 'I knew it! Tell me where it is, boy! And I'll give you this!' And from his flak jacket pocket Percival Rugg triumphantly pulled out a half-eaten packet of stale-looking wine gums and waved them enticingly under Mungo's nose.

'Wine gums!' scoffed Mungo. 'You think I'm going to sell the secret of St. Saviour's for a packet of manky old *wine gums* ? Dream on, Mr Rugg!' Mungo waved his list in the air. 'Even if you gave me everything I've written down here, I *still* wouldn't tell you. The location is so obscure that a search on the internet drew a blank. It took me three whole weeks to find it. Three whole weeks stuck in the local library studying an atlas before I eventually found it and was allowed into St. Misbehaviour's.' Mungo gave the Inspector an incredulous look as he began to walk away. He couldn't believe what he'd almost done. 'You almost fooled me Mr Rugg. M*sss* Bicep was right. She said that you weren't to be trusted. There is no School of the Year Award is there?'

Percival Rugg smirked at Mungo's retreating figure. 'Of course there's not, you stupid boy,' he snapped icily. 'And even if there was, St. Saviour's certainly wouldn't win it. That place isn't a *proper* school. It's a holiday camp, a playground, an amusement centre. A f-f-fun-filled abomination of a place. It shouldn't be allowed.'

Percival Rugg then began to jump up and down angrily, his mud mask starting to crack. 'I hate the place! Hate it! *hate it!* HATE IT! I say!' he roared. 'And if it's the last thing I do, I'll close it down, with or without your help, Pinks!'

Mungo ran as fast as his legs would carry him through the woods, not stopping until he'd reached the path that led to the nature trail. He leant against a tree to catch his breath. He knew he'd had a lucky escape. He could have told Percival Rugg everything and got nothing in return.

Mungo closed his eyes for a moment, smiling to himself as a map of the world flashed into his mind and then zoomed in on *that* special place. He knew in his heart that this was one secret that even he must never, ever break.

Chapter 8

A Smashing Time

'My goodness, 7R, it looks like you've been even busier than me,' announced Miss Twine as she joined her class, gathered in the farmyard at the end of the nature trail. The children smiled back at their teacher, each of them laden with the ferns, flowers and armfuls of twigs they'd hastily picked up along the way back. 'And there was me and Alberta thinking that you'd escaped for the afternoon.' The skeleton, tucked under Miss Twine's arm, now had a daisy chain around her neck.

The Science teacher frowned and looked around the yard. 'I don't suppose you've seen Mr Rugg anywhere have you? Only I've been so engrossed with examining wildflowers and plants all day, I hardly noticed his absence.'

Kimberly shook her head adamantly. 'No, Miss. We haven't seen him.'

'All afternoon,' added Suzette.

'The nature trail was really great though, Miss,' said Kimberly.

'Really interesting,' remarked Suzette.

'We found something very strange along the way,' added Kimberly, who was carrying a bunch of wildflowers to take home to her mum.

'Yeah, a real creepy crawly.' Suzette smiled knowingly at her friend.

'But don't worry 'cause we left it in the woods,' concluded Kimberly.

The rest of the class giggled as Miss Twine pointed towards the duck pond where a tractor lay half-submerged on its side. 'Oh dear. It looks like there's been some sort of an accident,' she sighed. 'Well, at least it can't be anything thing to do with St. Saviour's this time,' she said gratefully, remembering their visit to the Science museum when Stamford had accidentally smashed a valuable specimen jar. She turned her attention towards Benjy, who, she noticed, was carrying a chicken under his arm.'Benjy. What *are* you doing with that bird?' she asked sharply.

Benjy grinned back. 'I saved it, Miss,' he proudly declared.

Miss Twine raised an eyebrow sceptically. 'What from? A fox?' she asked dryly.

Benjy shook his head and tenderly stroked the chicken. 'No. From that pile of washing over there.' He pointed towards a broken washing line and the mass of garments scattered beneath it. 'It got caught up in some underwear, the poor thing. It must have been very frightened. Anyway, I untangled it and now I'm going to take it home with me,' said Benjy happily. 'I've never owned a pet before, 'cause my mum and step-dad don't like animals. In fact, they don't even like me very much,' he added dejectedly.

7R looked at Benjy sympathetically and Bop patted him on the shoulder.

'I don't think taking a chicken back to the city is such a good idea,' Miss Twine said kindly. 'But I'll tell you what we'll do. How about if I take a picture of you both together and you can keep it by your bedside as a memento?'

Benjy considered this option for a moment, and even though he didn't actually have a bed, let alone anything beside it, he nodded. 'OK. Perhaps you're right. I reckon it'll probably be happier roaming free than living in my cramped house anyway. It'll be safer here as well, cause my mum and step-dad would probably want to cook it for supper.'

Crystal stepped forward with an expensive camera. 'You can use this if you like,' she said, coyly glancing at Lee Topper to see if he looked impressed by her generosity. Lee didn't and he wasn't. He was too busy working out how he could avoid sitting next to Crystal on the ride back home.

Miss Twine took the camera and then took a snap of Benjy proudly holding the chicken aloft. Then she took a few more shots of the whole class, including Mungo who arrived just in time to stick his head in the frame.

Suddenly, from inside the farmhouse there came the sound of Stamford Nicks' raucous laughter. It sounded like a cross between the crashed tractor's engine and an excited seal. A moment later, both he and Beasley stepped outside along with the farmer, minus his pitchfork, thankfully.

'Anyway, thanks a lot for the lunch,' announced Beasley. 'And for telling us all about M*sss* Bicep when she was younger.' He stared shamefully towards the tractor. 'We're sorry about the accident as well. I hope you can get it fixed.'

'No problem,' replied the farmer. 'I was very angry when I saw that you'd stolen—'

'Er, borrowed actually,' Stamford butted in. 'My mum and dad always say that stealing is actually borrowing. The only difference being, you don't exactly know *when* you're going to give it back.'

'*Borrowed* my tractor then,' said the farmer hastily. 'But when I found out that you knew M*sss* Bicep-Tricep then obviously I had to let you off.' The man shook his head in admiration. 'I'm telling you, that woman is a saint. She's been coming to my farm for her annual holiday for years and last winter when I was having a particularly hard time, she gave me all her life savings to tide me over.'

The children and Miss Twine gathered around. 'That sounds like M*sss* B. She's helped me out of a bad situation before as well,' Benjy piped up, remembering the time his horrible mum and even more appalling step-dad had made him leave school to get a crummy job in a back-street barber's. He breathed a sigh of relief as he watched the chicken roaming around the yard. It had had a lucky escape. They'd have probably found it a job as well!

'Stamford, why are you holding a box of eggs and who's that photo of?' asked Mungo light-heartedly. He was feeling very guilty about having nearly destroyed the school and was trying to keep a low profile.

Stamford scowled. 'No thanks to you, Mung-Ears, but Mr Ravenshaw here has given me half a dozen free-range eggs and a snapshot of a cow for me mum.' Stamford held out the picture. 'I told him all about my dad wanting me to borrow a cow for me Mum's birthday present. So he's let me adopt one instead. Her name's Tracey. Sweet, innit?'

Beasley stared up at his friend in disbelief as Benjy thought to himself that he could do the same thing with the chicken. Perhaps they could be penpals? 'Cor. You've change your tune about cattle, Stamford,' Beasley declared, shaking his head. 'A few hours ago you were scared stiff of them.'

Stamford threw him an angry look as 7R tried not to laugh. 'Cows I don't mind,' sniffed Stamford haughtily. 'But there's something about sheep—' he peered tentatively over the wall of a pigsty, just in case one was lurking, ready to pounce. 'There's something about sheep that I'll never like.' He gazed at Mungo. 'They're a bit like you, Mung-Ears. Shifty, untrustworthy and peculiar to look at!'

Mungo looked away, shamefaced. If

Stamford knew the truth about what he'd been up to, his life wouldn't be worth living when they got back home – if he ever got back home.

'Anyway, class. We really need to be making a move soon,' declared Miss Twine. 'I've some urgent experiments waiting for me back at the laboratory and I'm also keen to see whether I can actually turn grass blue. I think it can be done,' the Science teacher said eagerly. 'What you do is …'

However, her scientific theories fell on deaf ears as the class began to wander off. No one shared Miss Twine's passion for Science, except Chester and even he had abandoned Physics for the afternoon in the pursuit of *lurrve*.

'We're just going to visit the gift shop before we leave, Miss,' Crystal called out, as Chester hurried after her and the rest of the class like a lovesick puppy.

'Well don't be long. I've a dissection awaiting me!' the Science teacher called after them irritatedly. She didn't care for souvenirs and trinkets. Miss Twine was only interested in things that you could cut up and examine.

The gift shop itself was tiny but somehow the whole class managed to squeeze inside. 'Only two schoolchildren at a time, the sign on the door clearly states,' snapped the tiny woman behind the tiny counter.

Stamford loomed over her like a giant in some miniature land. 'Got any tractors?' he enquired.

The little lady gave him a withering look. 'Now how on earth would we fit a tractor into a shop this size?' she snapped shrilly. 'There's not enough room to swing the farm's cat in here.'

The teeny woman didn't like tourists, especially schoolchildren. They dripped ice cream everywhere, mucked up her displays and got greasy finger marks all over the 'I've Been To Little Twitterings' bone-china tea services. Sometimes they even stole things.

She eyed the enormous boy standing before her suspiciously. He certainly had the look of a shoplifter about him. She could usually tell. It was the way their fingers flitted over the souvenirs, especially the expensive ones.

'I'm not after a real tractor,' said Stamford, his big fingers hovering above the solid silver 'A Present From Little Twitterings' fountain pens. 'I want a toy one for me baby bruvver, Filbert. I'd like him to 'ave a reminder of his big brother's day down on the farm. When he's older I can tell him all about the time I nicked – I mean borrowed – a tractor to escape some killer sheep.'

The tiny lady regarded him sceptically. 'Well, we've no tractors, not even miniature ones,' she replied curtly. 'But how about one of these instead?' And from beneath the counter she pulled out a stuffed fluffy toy.

Stamford's eyes widened in dismay as once again he came face to face with his worst nightmare: a sheep.

'It even makes a noise as well, listen!' said the petite shopkeeper. She pulled its tail and the sheep bleated.

DEADLY

'Get that thing away from me,' spluttered Stamford, backing away and stumbling over his classmates.

'Oi! Watch it, Stamford,' grumbled Lee who was trying to lose Crystal as she followed him doggedly around and around the glass display cabinets. It was proving impossible to avoid her, every time he turned around there she was, batting her eyelashes at him.

'Let me out of here!' hollered Stamford in a panic. 'THIS IS THE GIFT SHOP FROM HELL!' He whirled around, his mind racing. It seemed that everywhere he turned now, there were flocks of sheep staring at him from every direction. There were pictures of them on everything from postcards to tea towels. Stamford squealed as he also spotted a gold sheep-shaped pendant dangling off the jewellery stand.

The burly boy began to sweat as he made a dash for the door, his huge trainers kicking over a display stand in his desperate bid to escape. This in turn knocked over another stand, which knocked over another. 7R huddled in the corner and watched as ornaments toppled over like skittles and crashed to the floor. The noise was tremendous, louder than Stamford's

LITTLE
TWITTERINGS
APRIL
LITTLE
TWITTERINGS

clanking jewellery collection as he fled out of the shop in a whirlwind of purple, orange and gold.

'Whatever's happened, Stamford?' said Miss Twine, hurrying towards him.

Stamford pointed towards the shop. 'Don't go in there, Miss,' he panted. 'It's 'orrible.'

Miss Twine quickly walked over to the small shop front and peered in through the tiny window, shaking her head despairingly at the sight that met her eyes: a wrecked interior and a tiny, grim-faced assistant glaring back, holding a small sheep.

'Oh dear, Stamford. *More* breakages, I see,' sighed Miss Twine, entering the shop and tiptoeing her way across the broken glass to clean up the mess.

The tiny assistant put down the sheep and picked up a dustpan and brush, handing it to the Science teacher in angry silence. Miss Twine stared at the implement, thinking that perhaps she should have brought her microscope along, because even that seemed very small as well!

Half an hour later and two hundred and fifty-six pounds and eight pence lighter, Miss Twine was back on the coach, eager to be off.

'You know that shop assistant was extremely angry with you, Stamford,' the Science teacher said, settling Alberta into her seat and plonking a pot of clotted cream on to the skeleton's lap. 'It took me ages to calm her down. I've promised her that we won't ever come back, at least not to her gift shop anyway.'

Stamford shrugged nonchalantly. He was used to being banned from places. After all, back home he was forbidden from entering the park, the chip shop, the baker's, the petrol station and the ice rink.

'I don't care, Miss,' he replied, twiddling a solid silver pen (that he'd *borrowed* from the gift shop) between his nifty fingers. 'I've decided that I ain't ever coming back to the countryside. Not unless they build some amusement arcades out here and ban sheep.'

Miss Twine ignored her clumsy pupil's remarks as she pulled her leather bag down from the luggage rack and rummaged through it. 'Ah! This is what I'm looking for!' she announced eagerly, pulling out a small magnifying eye-piece and positioning it over her right eye.

'What's that for, Miss?' asked

P. RUGG

Benjy.

'For this!' beamed Miss Twine, triumphantly pulling a tiny lilac-coloured stone from her lab-coat pocket. 'I noticed it lying on the floor when I was sweeping up and paid ten pounds for it. A bargain, I might add, because I think it might be a brinestone rhinestone minestone – extremely rare, and worth a great deal of money.'

Stamford scowled, wishing that he'd *borrowed* that little rock instead.

The driver turned round in his seat and looked across at the Science teacher. 'We ought to be leaving now, Miss Twine, if we want to avoid the rush-hour traffic.'

Miss Twine didn't reply. She'd put in her ear-plugs and was scrutinizing the stone. 'Fascinating! Fascinating!' she mumbled over and over again, completely engrossed in her find.

'I reckon you ought to go, mate,' Stamford said. 'Once Miss Twine starts studyin' something, it'd take a herd of elephants to distract her.'

The driver looked round the coach. 'Are you sure there's no one left behind?'

'No, we're all here,' Bop called out.

'What about the other teacher though,' said the driver. 'Mr Rugg?'

'Oh, it's OK. He went home earlier,' Bop replied hastily. 'He wasn't feeling too well. I think it was a combination of coach sickness, countryside sickness and kid sickness,' he added with a smile.

The driver shrugged. 'Well, if you're quite sure, then we'd better be off.'

'Oh we're *quite* sure, Mister,' replied Bop. 'Mr Rugg was definitely feeling under the weather the last time we spoke to him.'

'Did you all have a good time today?' asked the driver as they headed out of the village.

'Smashing!' said Beasley, finishing off the last of his pick 'n' mix bag.

'Is that supposed to be funny?' growled Stamford, who was sitting beside him.

Beasley shook his head and turned his face away trying not to laugh as on the back seat Crystal Bow squeezed herself in between Lee Topper and Chester Heinz. The pampered pupil made herself comfortable and then handed Lee a carrier bag.

'What's this?' asked Lee dismissively.
'It's a present,' said Crystal excitedly. 'I couldn't resist. It reminded me of you.'

Chester sat on the other side of her looking crestfallen, wishing that he'd had the bright idea of buying Crystal Bow a gift. He did have a purchase in his pocket, but he didn't think that Crystal would take too kindly to being given a book entitled *A Young Scientist's Guide to Identifying Woodlice*.

Lee opened the bag grudgingly and looked inside. 'It's a toy sheep!' he cried, before closing the bag quickly and looking extremely embarrassed.

'I know,' trilled Crystal. 'Isn't it just the sweetest thing. Like I told you, Lee, I bought it because it reminds me of you. Cute to look at, completely irresistible and hard to catch!'

Lee Topper sank down in his seat and scowled out of the window. It was going to be a long, long, journey home.

Halfway up the coach Stamford frowned uneasily in his seat. He must be hearing things. He could have sworn that someone had just shouted out that dreaded word – sheep.

Chapter 9
Beast On A Bicycle

It was dawn in the idyllic village of Little Twitterings and a light fog hovered above the grass verges and coiled around the sleepy cottages. All was quiet.

Through the mist a figure emerged, stumbling up the lane. It was a man: tall and skinny and carrying a notebook.

Mrs Small, the gift shop owner, was the first person to spot him. Taking in the morning milk from the doorstep of her tiny cottage the little woman dropped the bottles in shock as the figure lurched towards her.

He was a mess. His hair was matted with twigs and leaves, his face was caked in mud and the camouflage gear that he wore was torn and wet. He was muttering incoherently under his breath a phrase that sounded like, 'Destroy the school. Destroy the school. I must destroy the school.' Over and over again the figure repeated the strange hypnotic chant.

He stopped by Mrs Small's tiny garden gate and stared at her, his expression wild and deranged.

'Can I help you?' asked Mrs Small, who despite her size was afraid of nothing and no one. 'Are you lost?'

The figure nodded resentfully. 'I've been lost all night in the woods,' he wailed. 'Captured by those barbarians and left to fend for myself in the wilderness.'

Mrs Small scuttled down her garden path towards him. Nothing interesting ever happened when you worked in a gift shop the size of a shoebox, and this was really exciting.

'Well I must say you do look in a sorry state,' she said, sounding thrilled. 'Perhaps you'd better sit down for a moment.' She indicated towards a bench in her garden but the man declined.

'How can I think about relaxing at a time like this!' he blustered. The figure's beady eyes darted about fearfully. 'Not when there's a school out there that's so vile and so wretched it must be destroyed!'

Mrs Small shook her head with

concern. 'Oh dear, you *are* upset. Perhaps you'd like me to call someone? A friend perhaps? What's your name?'

'My name, dear lady, is Percival Rugg,' snapped the Inspector crossly. 'And I have no friends, only enemies.' His eyes narrowed and his expression hardened even more. 'I need to get back to the school. I need transport and I need it now!'

Mrs Small checked her miniature wristwatch. 'Well, it is very early,' she announced. 'The first bus out of here doesn't leave for two hours and I can't give you a lift because I don't drive. How about a bite to eat whilst you wait for the bus?' she suggested, reluctant to let this strange man go. After all, this was the most exciting thing to happen in Little Twitterings since an American tourist had locked himself in the car park lavatories last summer.

Percival Rugg glared at her. 'Food! Who needs food, woman? I'm living on nothing but fresh air at the moment. It's vengeance that keeps me going. Vengeance and justice. I'M A D.U.B. MAN!' roared Percival Rugg, leaping up on to the garden wall. 'AND I WILL NEVER BE DEFEATED!'

Mrs Small gazed up at him, enthralled. She had no idea what D.U.B. stood for but she thought it sounded wildly exciting and possibly, judging by the man's attire, something to do with the military.

'There is one mode of transport that you could borrow,' suggested the diminutive woman helpfully. 'If you hold on I'll just nip and get it.'

Percival Rugg watched coldly as Mrs Small hurried back up the path and disappeared into her garage, returning a moment later wheeling along a rusty bicycle.

'Is that it?' seethed Percival Rugg. 'You're offering me a child's bicycle to ride home on?'

Mrs Small stared at him indignantly. 'It's not a child's. It's mine!' she snapped crossly. 'It's a bike built for a very small adult like myself actually. Why don't you hop on? Give it a go,' she said brightly. 'Look, it's even got a bell so everyone will know you're coming,' said Mrs Small eagerly.

Percival Rugg jumped down off the wall. He knew he had no option. He scowled as he climbed on. He didn't want anyone to see him coming on this ridiculous contraption. Then he rode it tentatively around the garden a few times, hunched over the handlebars with his knees knocking against them, before peddling out of the gate and up the lane. He made a mental note …

Ban small buildings, small two-wheeled vehicles and small people.

Mrs Small waved at his retreating figure wobbling from side to side on the rickety machine. 'Goodbye, Mr Rugg!' she called out. 'It was nice to meet you. And good luck with whatever it is that you're doing!'

Percival Rugg didn't reply. His mind was set on the road ahead.

The road to victory.

Chapter 10

The Beast Is Back

'Hogan Bathgate! Will you please come away from the window?' Miss Twine, brandishing her scalpel ready for the morning's Science lesson, frowned at her pupil. She knew that Hogan was one of life's dreamers and he was always staring out of windows. However, he'd been gazing out of this particular one for ten whole minutes now.

Hogan turned to face the teacher. 'Sorry, Miss. I was watching Mr Rugg coming up the road. He's just arrived in the playground now – on a bike. At least I think it's him. It could be the creature from the black lagoon.'

The whole class and Miss Twine hurried over to the window where down below they could see the distinctive figure of the Geography teacher peddling furiously across the playground.

'He's very late for classes this morning,' declared Miss Twine critically, glancing at the clock on the laboratory wall. 'I wonder where he's been?'

The children shrugged. Miss Twine still hadn't twigged that they'd left him behind yesterday. When they'd arrived for their lesson, she'd been totally absorbed a book called *The Science of Cheese,* whilst boiling some clotted cream in a test-tube.

Everyone glanced out of the window again at Mr Rugg, who had now abandoned his bike and was striding determinedly towards the entrance to the school. He was holding a camera and a notebook and he looked extremely upset.

Miss Twine frowned. 'Mr Rugg looks as if he's spent the night in a ditch.'

The students of 7R lowered their eyes. For a moment, nobody spoke. But then Benjy, who was used to getting into trouble at home, said shamefully, 'Actually, Miss. We've got a confession to make. Mr Rugg had to camp out last night, because we left him in the woods.'

Miss Twine regarded her class sternly. 'The whole school is aware that Mr Rugg is a spy. However, leaving him to fend for himself all

'A night in the wilderness isn't very charitable, is it? Here at St. Saviour's we don't encourage our pupils to tell lies, except when really necessary, of course,' she added hastily, 'or to be mean to other people.' She tapped her scalpel briskly on her desk and gazed at her pupils confrontingly. 'Now tell me the truth. Did you capture him?'

Bop looked up and nodded begrudgingly. 'Yes, Miss Twine, we did. It was my idea. We captured him and hung him upside down in the woods by his feet. I don't know how he could have escaped. He was very securely tied.'

Mungo sank down on his chair, wishing the ground would swallow him up as Chester put up his hand.

'It wasn't just Bop's idea. I was in on the plan as well.' He pushed his glasses up his nose agitatedly as Miss Twine listened to Chester's confession, along with the rest of the class as they all began to own up to their deeds. When they'd finished telling Miss Twine all about the rat-trap idea and how they'd built it, 7R sat back and waited for her reaction.

Miss Twine shook her head and picked up a leaf from her desk, studying it intently.

'Do you think she's angry?' hissed Benjy to Bop. 'She's gone awfully quiet.'

Bop Stevens shrugged and stared back at his teacher as a smile slowly began to flicker across her face.

Miss Twine looked up. 'Brilliant! Quite, quite brilliant!' she beamed. 'I'm proud of you, 7R. Last week's lesson on force and gravity obviously made an impression on you. And there was me thinking that you never paid any attention in class!'

7R grinned back at her. Miss Twine was right. They didn't ever listen to her. Once again it had been Chester and his vast knowledge who'd had been the brains behind the operation.

'Do you have the drawings, Chester?' asked Miss Twine eagerly. 'I'd love to see the construction.' Any glimmer of sympathy that she'd had for Percival Rugg was long gone, now that the subject of Science was involved.

Chester shook his head. 'They were only sketches, Miss. I left them back at the camp.'

Before Miss Twine could ask any more probing questions the classroom door flew open and there standing in the doorway was the muddy figure of Percival Rugg.

'SURPRISE!' he announced shrilly. 'Bet you thought you'd seen the last of old Percy?'

'Ah Mr Rugg! The children have just been telling me about your capture,' said Miss Twine brightly. 'I know it was a bit naughty of them, but you really do have to admire their ingenuity.'

'I don't admire anything about kids,' snapped Percival Rugg. 'Can't stand the little creatures,' he glared at the astonished Science teacher before striding into the room and surveying the children coldly. 'What's the matter? Aren't you pleased to see your *Geography* teacher?' he asked drolly.

Bop and Benjy looked at each other disbelievingly. What was it with the Rugg Rat? He just kept on bouncing back.

Percival Rugg began to stroll around the classroom. 'Right, 7R. The f-f-party's over,' he stuttered, in a cold and calculating voice. 'You lot think you're clever, don't you?' He stopped behind Bop's chair and leant towards him. 'But I'm cleverer.'

Bop scowled as Percival Rugg's clammy breath wafted up his nose. Then the Inspector stood up. 'Bet you didn't bargain on old Percy having a camera though did you? Hmm?'

7R stared up at him grudgingly as the phoney teacher waved the camera in the air.

'I've got a film in here of the camp and its contents, including the sketches that you made, Chester Heinz.' He stared at Chester who blinked nervously back at him through his spectacles. 'You should have been brainier Chester, and destroyed the evidence.'

Bop put up his hand. 'Why didn't you just bring them back with you, then?' he asked suspiciously.

Percival Rugg giggled. 'What? With my track record for holding on to pieces of paper? Not a chance, sonny. They could have fallen into enemy hands – or paws,' he added, thinking of Deadly who wasn't around, he noticed with relief. 'And then I'd have been back to square one. I'm taking this film to be developed and nothing is going to stop me!' Percival Rugg marched over to the door and turned around. 'I'd start packing now if I were you children, because by this time tomorrow you'll all be at Chaste High!' And he raced up the corridor, his maniacal laughter and dreaded words ringing in the children's ears.

'Oh this is marvellous news, Mrs Small,' enthused Percival Rugg, as he paced up and down the pavement talking to the gift shop owner on his mobile phone. 'And you say you tracked me down through the phone directory? Well, that's amazing because I didn't know the D.U.B. was even listed. And you've told my secretary that you're willing to testify to my superiors that these particular children wrecked your shop?'

Percival Rugg was beside himself with excitement. Mrs Small had called him out of the blue as he was waiting outside the photographic shop. She'd said that she hadn't been able to stop thinking about him and had decided to track him down.

'Well, of course you can have your

bike back, Mrs Small,' continued Percival Rugg, his mind racing as he imagined every door and window of St. Saviour's boarded up, with an armed guard patrolling it as an added precaution. 'Can I bring it in person? Well, I'll have to see how busy I am. Buildings to close down. Lives to wreck. You know how it is. However, just let me close this case once and for all and then I'll be in touch. Goodbye.'

'Wotcha, Mr Rugg. Who was that on the dog and bone? Yer girlfriend?'

The Inspector whirled around and came face to face with Stamford Nicks and Beasley grinning at him. Percival Rugg looked down at the ground, and clutched his phone protectively as Deadly looked up at him, eyeing it hungrily.

'Why aren't you in school?' snapped the Inspector. 'While you still can be,' he added with a smirk.

'I've been to the er, dentist,' frowned Stamford, once again using the one and only excuse that he had for truancy. 'And wot do you mean by "while you still can"?'

Percival stared at him languidly and made a mental note ...

Nicks boy spends far too much time at the dentist. Must be all the sweet, sticky desserts that are served up at lunchtimes. Make certain that those homicidal calorie-loving dinner ladies never work in the catering profession again.

'The game's up, boys,' announced Percival Rugg. He checked his watch. 'In approximately three minutes my Little Twitterings field trip photos will be developed and I will have all the evidence that I need to close your little playpen down! Plus—' Percival Rugg held up a finger triumphantly, 'I now have the added bonus of an informant.'

Stamford looked at him huffily. 'Who is it? Mung-Ears, I suppose?' he declared morosely. 'Wait till I get me hands on that little grass.'

Percival Rugg shook his head. 'No, it's not Mungo Pinks. Although that child was going to work for me, he lost his nerve when I asked him the whereabouts of Qing Zang. No. I have a far more reliable source now.'

'Oh yeah and who's that then?' asked Beasley sniffily.

'If I say the words "gift shop" and

"destroyed", would that ring any bells?' smirked Percival Rugg.

'Wot? You don't mean that little woman who scared me with the stuffed sheep, do yer?' asked Stamford.

Percival Rugg nodded enthusiastically. 'The very same. Mrs Small.'

'I knew there was somethin' shifty about her,' said Stamford sulkily. 'Apart from bein' the world's shortest woman, her eyes were too close together.' Stamford shuddered. 'And her shop was really creepy, all those pictures of sheep everywhere. It's unhealthy.'

'Well I could stand around chatting all day, but I don't want to,' replied Percival Rugg sarcastically. 'Like I told your classmates earlier, you'd better get your things together, because this time tomorrow St. Saviour's will be history.' Percival Rugg glanced at his watch again. 'Now if you'll excuse me boys, I think my evidence should just about be ready.' He stared coldly at Beasley and Stamford. 'I'd like to say that it's been nice knowing you, but I can't. Goodbye.'

And with that he hurried into the shop. Meanwhile, Stamford, Beasley and Deadly – who was delighted to be reunited with his best buddy – ran across the road and jumped on to the first bus that was heading out of town. They had no time to lose. They had to get back to school. M*sss* Bicep-Tricep needed to be informed about these developments. It would appear that the Rugg Rat was winning and that would never do.

Chapter 12

Pastures New

The sounds of Percival Rugg's sobs coming from inside the Say Cheese photo processing shop were so loud they could be heard all the way up the High Street. Inside the shop the Inspector, who had collapsed in a heap against the counter, was banging his fist slowly on the top of it and sobbing uncontrollably. In his other hand he was clutching some glossy photographs. All of them were blank.

'But there must be some mistake!' wailed Percival Rugg, his mud- and tear-stained faced staring imploringly up at the assistant. 'I need those prints!'

The young man shook his head, recognizing this character from the mobile phone shop that he'd worked in before getting the sack for calling his mates on the latest stock. The assistant also noticed with some alarm how much the man had deteriorated in a matter of weeks.

'I'm afraid there's no mistake. I've spoken to the manager and he says it would appear that you forgot to take the lens cap off, which is why the pictures never came out.' The youth shrugged as Percival Rugg blubbered all over the counter. 'Sorry about that. But at least you've still got your mobile phone,' he added breezily.

Percival Rugg wiped his face and gathered himself together. 'Yes. And at least I've still got my informant as well,' he sniffed. 'No. I mustn't crumble, all is not lost. I shall return to St. Saviour's and inform the Head that the battle is over.' He slapped the blank pictures down on the counter. 'After all, the spoken word is far deadlier than a few snapshots,' he announced soberly.

The assistant nodded blankly as the Chief Inspector turned and marched out on to the busy street. He kept on marching, his expression resolute beneath his muddy mask and he didn't stop until he'd reached the school gates.

*

'He's back, M*sss* Bicep-Tricep,' said Benjy Butler, poking his head around the Head Teacher's office door. 'Thank you, Benjy. Send him straight up and then go and wait in the common room. I'll call you all when the coast is clear,' replied M*sss* Bicep-Tricep, swinging from side to side in her high wing-backed chair.

Benjy gave her the thumbs up and then headed back down the stairs. M*sss* Bicep-Tricep stubbed out her cigar and smiled to herself before setting to work. First she turned down the horse racing on her portable TV set and then she pulled out a mammoth address book from the drawer of her desk. Cynthia Bicep-Tricep was an extremely popular woman and it was the thickness of a phone directory.

'Now where's her number?' she muttered, scanning the pages with her long, perfectly manicured fingernail and stroking Bobby, one of her beloved toads, with the other hand. She flipped over the page and glanced up at the door. Percival Pugg would be here any minute and she needed to get her timing just right. 'Scotch, Sheldon, Sidney – Oh, I haven't spoken to Nanette Sidney for years!' trilled M*sss* Bicep-

Tricep, running her finger quickly down the long list. 'Slater, ah here we are, Bobby – Marcia Small. Little Twitterings 55255,' she declared jubilantly. Then she quickly dialled the number. After a moment her call was answered. 'Marcia? It's Cynthia! … Yes I know, long time no speak! How are you, darling? … Listen, what's all this about you and a certain gentleman called Percival Rugg?'

Outside in the corridor, with his ear pressed firmly up against the office door Percival Rugg listened intently. He couldn't believe what he was hearing. Mrs Small best pals with M*sss* Bicep-Tricep? Surely not? The Chief Inspector bit his knuckles in frustration, trying not to cry out as the conversation continued.

'Now listen, Marcia, my pupils have come clean. They've told me all about the little accident. Yes. I know they made a mess, but Marcia, think about it. Even you were young once! … Well, that's very kind of you, dear. So you'll forget the whole thing? Splendid! … No, I don't think Percival Rugg's handsome and widow or not, Marcia, I don't think he'd make a suitable boyfriend for you! You really need to go and get your eyes tested. If you're looking for a suitable suitor, why not try Charlie Ravenshaw at the farm? I've heard he even does his own washing! Anyway, I'll be down for a visit at the weekend so I'll put in a good word for you if you like. See you in a few days. Bye-bye dear.' M*sss* Bicep-Tricep leant back in her chair and lit another cigar triumphantly.

'Come in, Mr Plugg,' she announced with a smile. Percival Rugg blustered in, his fists clenched, glaring like a mad man at the Head Teacher. 'Take a seat Mr Zugg. You look positively worn out.' M*sss* Bicep-Tricep indicated towards a chair.

Percival Rugg's nose twitched as her cigar smoke wafted under it. 'Is there no one that you don't happen to be friends with?' he seethed, standing in front of her desk.

M*sss* Bicep-Tricep shrugged and flicked her ash nonchalantly into an 'I've Been to Little Twitterings' ashtray. 'Being nice is important, Mr Mugg,' she announced, arching a heavily pencilled eyebrow at him. 'You should try it some time.'

Percival Rugg glowered at her through the smoke and then glanced up at the wall behind her. 'W-w-who took th-th-

that?' he demanded, pointing to a framed photograph above her head. This was more than he could bear. It was a perfect picture, in focus and beautifully lit, showing a smiling Benjy Butler holding the chicken aloft with 7R surrounding him. Below it was printed 'Hero of the Day'.

M*sss* Bicep-Tricep waved her cigar languidly towards it. 'Miss Twine took it. Isn't it wonderful? I just had to get a copy framed as a reminder of my dear pupils.'

Percival Rugg advanced towards the desk and then backed off hastily as M*sss* Bicep-Tricep gave him one of her infamous withering looks. 'Don't come any closer Mr Smugg,' she remarked dryly. 'I have an aversion to spoilsports.'

The Inspector frowned as a moment later from beneath her desk a soft clucking sound could be heard. 'What was that?' snapped Percival Rugg. 'It sounded like a chicken.'

'Right first time, Mr Fugg,' announced the Head Teacher, reaching under her desk and lifting a small brown chicken from beneath it. She placed it on the desk proudly. 'Benjy Butler isn't allowed pets at home. So it got me thinking.' She gazed at Percival Rugg indifferently. 'St. Saviour's is going to expand, Mr Jugg.'

The Chief Inspector shook his head slowly. 'Expand!' he blustered. 'You can't EXPAND! This place is listed for closure, not DEVELOPMENT!'

M*sss* Bicep-Tricep stood up and walked

over to the window. 'We're branching out, Mr Thugg and neither you nor your horrible little organization can stop us. I'm taking over that wasteground in front of the school and I'm going to build a farm on it,' she announced proudly.

'A FARM!' bellowed Percival Rugg. 'In the middle of the city!' He paced up and down the office carpet, tugging at his sparse hair, his mind in turmoil as the Head Teacher continued.

'Yes. We'll start with a few chickens – maybe a cow. A few pigs, perhaps. But strictly no sheep on Stamford Nicks' request.' M*sss* Bicep-Tricep sighed contentedly. 'If St. Saviour's can't get to the countryside, then it's up to me to bring a bit of the countryside to St. Saviour's.' She turned and faced Percival Rugg. 'Benjy Butler isn't the only pupil at St. Saviour's who isn't allowed a pet you know, Mr Glugg. So this will be the ideal opportunity for those particular children to have one of their own here.'

Percival Rugg stared at her hatefully. 'You're mad,' he said. 'You won't get away with this! There must be regulations against having a smallholding in a built-up area!'

M*sss* Bicep-Tricep shrugged. 'On the contrary, Mr Bugg. You see, I own that patch of land already and I've got ten chickens, a shetland pony and a peacock all arriving next week.'

'A peacock!' blustered Percival Rugg, hardly believing his ears.

'Yes. To brighten up the place,' added M*sss* Bicep-Tricep happily.

'Right. That's it!' yelled the Inspector. 'I've had enough of this!'

'You mean you surrender, Mr Flugg?' asked the Head Teacher, sitting back down at her desk.

'NEVER!' bellowed Percival Rugg. He stamped his foot angrily before marching out of the office and slamming the door with such force Benjy's photograph almost fell off the wall.

M*sss* Bicep-Tricep stood up, adjusted it and then sat back down, a self-satisfied smile flickering across her lips. Then she reached forward and picked up a silver-grey notebook. 'Oh dear, Bobby. Mr Slugg was in such a hurry he forgot to take this with him,' she said. The toad croaked beside her as she slipped the book inside her desk drawer, lit another enormous cigar and turned towards the TV set. 'Ah good, Bobby. We're just in time,' she announced cheerfully, turning up the sound. 'The 4.15 at Uttoxeter is just about to start.'

Percival Rugg glared up at the school building as he made his way across the playground towards the school gates. It seemed as if the whole school had turned out to wave him off. Wherever he looked a sea of children's faces were grinning back at him from every open window.

'See you later, Mr Rugg. Maybe,' Bop Stevens called out from the upstairs common room.

'Did you hear about our farm?' Benjy Butler shouted down. 'Isn't it brilliant? M*sss* Bicep says I can be in charge of the chickens!'

Percival Rugg ignored their remarks and walked stiffly across the playground where the caretaker, Edwin Fox, was standing by the entrance, dressed in his usual attire – a dressing gown and embroidered silk slippers.

'Leaving us already Mr Rugg?' enquired the caretaker as he unlocked the gates.

Percival Rugg stared at him disdainfully as

he remembered the caretaker's ridiculous poems pinned up on the school noticeboard. Who'd ever heard of a mere *cleaner* writing poetry before? It shouldn't be allowed. He made a mental note as he stepped on to the pavement …

> Make sure all manual workers, cleaners, road sweepers, dinner ladies, etc are not allowed access to poetry, including Shakespeare.

'Are you coming back?' asked Edwin, putting the bunch of keys back in his dressing-gown pocket.

Percival Rugg nodded abruptly. 'Oh I'll be back all right,' he replied curtly. 'And it won't be on a bicycle this time, either!'

Edwin looked at him quizzically. He could feel a poem coming on. He'd call it *Bore on a Bike*. 'Oh. What will it be then?' asked Edwin casually.

'A BULLDOZER!' bellowed Percival Rugg as he hurried up the road. He still wasn't beaten. If he could just lay his hands on one of those gigantic machines he could single-handedly bulldoze that wretched school to the ground.

Percival Rugg sniggered as he imagined the children clambering over the pile of rubble in search of their belongings. They wouldn't be laughing at him then. Oh no! Not when their beloved St. Misbehaviour's was nothing but a heap of bricks. Chaste High probably wouldn't take them either. It was far too respectable. They'll be educational orphans with no where to go, he thought gleefully to himself. Percival Rugg stopped, put his hands on his hips and stood determinedly in the middle of the pavement. A few passers by stared at him strangely.

'I MUST! I MUST! I MUST DEMOLISH THE SCHOOL!' he bellowed at the top of his voice before heading off in search of the nearest building site.

Look out for more reckless reading from Hodder Children's Books ...

1: DISCO INFERNO

A tale of deception, discos and a dog called Deadly ...

When parents' night comes round, no one's afraid of lousy marks and bad reports – but what if the parents find out what the staff are really like? It's the perfect chance for ruthless Rugg to enact his evil scheme. If he succeeds, then class 7R will be destined to a fate worse than death –the perilously posh Chaste High . . .

2: ROMAN AROUND

A tale of terror, togas and Chinese takeaways ...

Class 7R is enjoying being Romans in a special History lesson at the local swimming baths when they discover the mystery of 'Wet Bob'. But a creepy poolside ghost is no threat compared to their tyrannical teacher, Mr Rugg – determined once again to pursue his appalling plan ...

Look out for more reckless reading from Hodder Children's Books ...

4: NO SURRENDER

A tale of sieges, shovels and shady dinner ladies ...

Percival Rugg has finally cracked. His superiors refuse to accept his claims about the scandalous school, so he's taking matters into his own horrible hands. When the bulldozers move in, Class 7R realizes this time drastic action is needed, and so the siege of St. Misbehaviour's begins ...